EMMA
IS ON THE AIR
#4: UNDERCOVER!

by IDA SIEGAL

illustrations by
KARLA PEÑA

SCHOLASTIC INC.

Text copyright © 2016 by Ida Siegal
Illustrations copyright © 2016 by Scholastic Inc.

This book is being published simultaneously in hardcover by Scholastic Press.

ISBN 978-0-545-68710-2

10 9 8 7 6 5 4 3   16 17 18 19 20

Printed in the U.S.A.   40

First printing 2016

Book design by Mary Claire Cruz

CONTENTS

CHAPTER
ONE

Snow Tag, So Mad!

THIS is Emma and I'm on the air!" I said into my camera phone as I stood in the school yard. "Time for the weather!"

It was so windy, my pudding Slinky curls were flying in the air behind me.

"It is really cold outside. Well, duh, you probably know that if you've been out of the house today. But here's how I know for sure . . ."

I tilted the camera down to show my glove.

"Look . . . My Freezy glove changed color!

The flower turned from yellow to hot pink. And the rainbow isn't gray anymore—it has all the colors. The rainbow only gets its colors when it's super cold out."

This was my first weather report because I decided I could do all kinds of news on my show. Not every story has to be a mystery investigation. Of course, mysteries are the most fun! Like when my news team found the missing tambora drum or when we found Sophia's stolen Lion costume. Even when we figured out how the worm got in Javier's wormburger, we had to do an investigation. We had to do interviews, find clues, and solve problems. Then we put it all in our news reports. Those were cool, but you know what? People also needed to know about things like the weather!

"Yes, it's definitely a cold one today," I said into my camera phone. "Freezy gloves don't lie!"

"And look—it's snowing!" Javier suddenly screamed, dashing behind me. He was right. Snow flurries started to fall all around us. I pointed the camera phone up to the sky to show the snow. Then I felt someone tap me on the shoulder.

"Tag—you're it!" shouted Adrian. He let out a sneaky laugh and ran off.

"Snow tag!" yelled Javier. Everyone started running around like crazy. I quickly pressed the send button on my phone. Just like that, my weather report went straight to the Internet. Papi taught me how to do that. He even gets a special alert when there's a new "Emma Is On the Air" story online.

I put my phone in my backpack and plopped it down next to the playground fence. Then I took off after Adrian. I couldn't let him snow-tag me and get away with it.

I ran as fast as I could to the other side of the school yard to catch up with him. Snow flurries were crashing into my face as I zoomed across. Adrian was too quick. His dirty-blond hair looked like a whizzing bumblebee, always out of reach. I saw Sophia hiding behind the tree to my right, so I decided to run after her instead.

"You're it, Sophia!!" I yelled as I tagged her elbow.

She laughed and screamed and then started running after Lizzie. Then Lizzie tagged Shakira, and Shakira tagged Molly, and Molly tagged Melissa G. Ugh. I didn't know Melissa G. was playing. I sped up to get away from Melissa G. I definitely didn't want her to catch me. Then she would spend the whole day talking about how fast she can run. She's so annoying.

I was zooming so fast to get away from Melissa, I finally caught up to Adrian. He smiled at me and then took off even faster. That made me run faster, too. We started to race. I never knew how speedy I could be! We zigzagged across the school yard together as the snow-flakes got bigger and bigger. It was so fun I started laughing uncontrollably—I even snorted. Ha! That's why I didn't notice when Melissa G. caught up to Adrian.

"Got ya, Adrian! You're it!" she yelled.

Then Adrian started chasing after Melissa. Suddenly I wasn't laughing anymore. I stopped running. I was feeling, well, just really mad. *I* was playing with Adrian. Why did Melissa have to tag him? Couldn't she tag someone else? Just then, Adrian ran over a small icy patch on the ground. He slipped and fell.

"Oww!!!" Adrian shrieked from the cold ground. He wrapped his arms around his knee. Ouch. That looked painful. I ran over to help.

Except instead of helping ... I just started to yell.

"Look what you did!" I yelled at Melissa. "Now Adrian is hurt all because of you!"

"That wasn't my fault!" Melissa yelled back. She looked angry and sad at the same time.

"Adrian, are you okay?" I asked. But before he could answer, I turned back to Melissa and said, "You ruined everything. We didn't even want to play tag with you anyway."

After I said that, my stomach felt weird. Like there was a big rock sitting in it. Like maybe I had gone too far. Maybe I said something too mean. But I wasn't sure what to do next. I looked up and noticed everyone was crowded around us. Staring. Melissa G. looked like she was going to cry.

"Um, Emma, that wasn't very nice," Sophia finally said.

"Yeah, and it's not true," added Molly. "*I* wanted Melissa G. to play."

It felt like everyone was against me. Even Adrian wasn't on my side.

"Yeah, it's cool, Emma. Look, I'm fine now," he said as he started to get up from the ground.

But Geraldine the lunch lady didn't think it was cool. She marched over to us.

"What's going on over here? Why is everyone standing around? Why was Adrian on the ground?" Geraldine said in her disapproving voice, with her hands on her hips.

"It's okay, I'm fine," said Adrian. Geraldine noticed the patch of ice next to him.

"Uh-oh. Icy already. This winter is a doozy. You sure you're okay, Adrian?"

"Yeah, I'm fine, I swear," he repeated.

Geraldine blew her whistle. "Everyone line

up! The rest of recess will be indoors. It's too icy and dangerous. Everyone line up to go inside."

Our group headed toward the cafeteria door. I walked over to pick up my backpack by the fence. I was still feeling angry and a little nervous. What just happened? Why did they all take Melissa's side? I mean, it was her fault! She's the one who made Adrian fall. Right?

I reached inside my purple sparkle backpack to make sure all my reporter tools were there. Everything was in place, so I put my backpack on and turned around to head back to the cafeteria with everyone else. But they were all gone. I was all alone in the school yard. I felt like a tiny pinecone in a big, empty forest. A little teardrop started to peek out of my eye. I ran inside before it could travel down my cheek.

CHAPTER
TWO

Mysterious Riddle

THE next morning, I was afraid to go to school. What if everyone was still mad at me?

Luna jumped on my lap at the kitchen table like always—but not even my soft chocolate-pudding kitty could cheer me up. I scratched her chin and stared at my cereal, wondering if I should tell my mom I wasn't feeling well. Yeah, maybe I was getting sick and should stay home from school today.

"Emma, you haven't touched your breakfast. The bus will be here soon. Let's boogie,"

Mom said from the other side of the kitchen as she put plates in the dishwasher. My little sister, Mia, was "helping" her. Every time Mom put a plate in, baby Mia took a cup out.

"But, Mom, how can I eat this cereal? It's gross! Besides, I'm not hungry anyway," I said, sulking.

"Okay. Then don't eat it. How about some fruit?" she offered.

"Fruit? You want me to eat fruit? Ugh!" I yelled back. I felt so frustrated! But I wasn't sure why. Suddenly my mom had that look like maybe she was concerned.

"Hey, hey . . . ¿Qué pasa, mija?" Papi said, walking into the kitchen. "What's going on? Why are you speaking to your mother like that?"

"Forget it, Papi. You wouldn't understand," I replied. I put my head down in my arms on the table. I just wanted to be left alone.

"I'm your *papi*—try me."

"Well, this cereal is bad," I explained with my head still down. "And I hate fruit." I lifted my head up and put my hand on my forehead. "And I think I'm getting sick. And I don't want to go to school. Besides everyone hates me anyway."

"Okay, slow down, *mija*," Papi said as Mom put her hand on my forehead to feel my temperature.

"You don't feel warm," she said. "What happened at school?"

I wasn't sure if I should tell Mom and Papi what happened. But Papi gave me that look like I didn't have a choice. So I told them all about what Melissa G. did in the school yard and how I yelled at her. And then how everybody got mad at me instead of her.

"Yes, that would make me upset, too," said

Papi after I finished. "It doesn't feel good when we hurt other people, does it?"

"No," I replied, looking at the floor.

"There's an easy solution," Mom said. "Just apologize to Melissa G. You'll feel much better."

"Apologize?? But she's the one who made Adrian slip . . . and she's the one who—"

Papi interrupted me. "We know, Emma. But you said some hurtful things. You owe her an apology. That's all."

"Fine," I said.

"I know you can do it. You are brave. You are kind. And your friends love you. Don't worry," Mom added.

"Okay," I said, still sulking. I wasn't sure if they were right about this.

"Looks like we missed the school bus," Papi said as he stood up. "Grab a granola bar, and I'll drive you to school."

By the time I got to school, our class was lining up. We had library first thing that morning. I looked for my friends in line, and I saw Adrian and Melissa G. paired together. They were talking about something. It must have been something hilarious because they were both laughing. Behind them, I saw Sophia and Javier, and they were laughing, too. What was so funny?

I started to feel mad all over again. They were probably all laughing at me. Or maybe they were making plans to play at recess without me. I walked past them all and stood in the back of the line by myself. We walked down the hall to the school library, and I was still feeling mad. And sad. And also just so . . . so . . . mad. It wasn't *fair*.

"Come inside, everyone," said Mrs. Myrtle, the school librarian. "This week we're going to look for books about sea animals. I know you're studying the occan in science. I've set aside some books on the back table that will work well, but you're welcome to browse on your own."

Everyone walked over to the back table to find a book about the ocean. I walked slowly behind them and then ducked into another aisle in the library. I wanted to be alone. I walked to the back corner near a window and started scanning the shelves. It felt like a good hiding place.

I decided to get down on my knees to inspect the books on the very bottom shelf. I bet no one ever paid attention to the books at the bottom. I felt bad for them. They must be lonely down there.

Kneeling close to the floor like that, I noticed something shiny. The light from the window was reflecting off it and shining in my eye. I moved some books aside so I could see clearly. I saw what looked like an old book stuck behind the shelf, under the radiator. The sunlight was reflecting off the gleaming, round award label on the cover. I stuck my arm behind the shelf until I could feel the book in my hand. I grabbed it and pulled it out, rescuing it from that cramped prison under the radiator.

The book was old and sticky and dusty. My hands felt grimy holding it. I could tell no one

had touched this book in a really long time. It must have fallen down there ages ago. How could people just forget about a book and leave it all alone? That's not nice. I decided I would take care of it since no one else had.

The title on the cover said *Bridge to Terabithia*. I'd never heard of that book before, but it looked like it might be famous. I traced my fingers over that shiny award seal on the cover. When I opened the cover, it made a creaking noise. I had to use my hand to wave away the dust cloud that floated up into my face.

On the inside was a pocket for the library checkout card. I pulled the card out and looked at it. Just like I thought: The last time this book was checked out was October 17, 2000.

I did the math in my head. That was more than fifteen years ago. Who read it? How did it get stuck behind the shelf? Next to the check-out date on the card was the name Sarah O. Spellman. Who was she? What was she like?

I tried to put the card back in the pocket, but it didn't fit. Something was blocking it. I looked inside the slot and realized there was a folded-up piece of paper there. I pulled the paper out and opened it up. It was a riddle.

A princess in a tower, locked away for years.
Please, someone save her. Don't mind her floppy ears.
I can't tell you more. You'll have to find the clues.
She's trapped across the way where the chirping babies snooze.
—Sarah Spellman, 30 Washington Way, Seattle, Washington

CHAPTER
THREE

A Princess in a Tower??

SARAH Spellman was the girl from the check-out card. She was the last person to read this book, and she left this note. But it said she lived in Seattle. Why would someone who lived in Seattle check out a book in New York City? And why did she leave this riddle? What was she talking about? What princess? What tower? It was all very strange. I figured it probably wasn't true. Princesses don't get locked in towers anymore. Not in real life. Right? But something told me I needed to figure out what it was all about.

"Emma?" called Mrs. Myrtle. She spotted me sitting on the floor and started walking toward me. I stood up with the book in my hand. I was about to explain what I discovered, but then it occurred to me—this might be an interesting news story. People might want to know about a lost book with a weird riddle.

"What are you doing here?" Mrs. Myrtle asked once she made it down the aisle. "I don't think there are any books about the ocean back here."

"I know. I'm sorry. But . . . I'm actually . . . working on a news story. Can I interview you?"

"Oh," she replied. "I guess so. So long as you choose an ocean book when we're done."

"I will," I promised.

"Okay, come to the other side of the room so I can keep an eye on the rest of the class."

We walked up to the front desk together. I noticed Javier and Sophia look up from their table. They probably wondered what I was doing. I ignored them.

I pulled out my camera phone and Emma microphone and pressed record.

"Mrs. Myrtle," I began, "I want to show you this book I found." I put my microphone under my arm so I could hand her the book. Then I grabbed it again and continued. "I noticed it in the back behind the shelf. It looks like it fell back there and was forgotten about. See the check-out card?"

Mrs. Myrtle opened the book, and another cloud of dust floated up. She scrunched up her nose and waved it away.

"Look at that, this book has been missing for quite some time. It looks like it was last checked out in 2000."

"Do you know who Sarah Spellman is?" I didn't want to tell Mrs. Myrtle about the riddle

Sarah left. She might think it was silly and throw it away or something.

"You know what—I do remember a Sarah Spellman. That was a *long* time ago. I'd just started working here at P.S. 387. I remember Sarah because she spent a lot of time in the library. She would sit here for hours reading books, almost always by herself. I worried she wasn't making friends. And then after fourth grade, her parents decided to move to Seattle. I never saw her again. I wonder what ever happened to her?"

"Sarah never made a lot of friends? That's really sad . . ." I said, thinking out loud.

"Yes, I tried to help her, but she said she just preferred to stay here and read by herself." Mrs. Myrtle looked down at the book again. "I don't remember her reading *Bridge to Terabithia . . .* although it makes sense. A book about two kids imagining a life away from the real world was just up her alley."

"Mrs. Myrtle, one more question." I held the microphone a bit closer to my mouth so I could whisper. I didn't want anyone else to hear. "Did Sarah ever talk to you about a princess locked up in a tower?"

"Um, not that I can recall. That's an odd question."

"Oh, never mind. Thanks, Mrs. Myrtle."

"Anytime, dear."

"Do you mind if I hang on to this book for a while? I think I might need it for my news story."

"I don't see why not. I still have to go

into the computer and make a record that it's been found after all these years. But make sure you take good care of it."

"I will. Thanks, Mrs. Myrtle."

"Now go get your ocean book."

"Okay."

I pressed stop on my phone and grabbed a book about the ocean from the back table. I was thinking about Sarah and how she had no friends. I kind of knew how that felt. Sarah must have written that riddle because she needed help and she didn't have any friends to talk to. It seemed a little silly to need help saving a princess in a tower. I couldn't help but feel like there was something more. She was trying to send a message—and no one got it because the book went missing.

But I got the message! I decided that *I* would be Sarah's friend. I would help her save the princess in the tower! Or whatever it was that needed saving.

I was about to form a plan when I noticed Javier, Sophia, and Shakira walk over to my table.

"Hey, Emma," Shakira began, "how come you haven't said hi to us today?"

"What's wrong?" asked Sophia.

"Yeah, you're acting strange," Javier added. "And if *I* think you're acting strange . . . then something really is wrong." He smirked.

I wasn't sure what to say. But they didn't seem mad at me anymore.

"I just didn't see you guys," I lied. "Everything's fine. Actually, I'm glad I found you—we have a new case!"

I decided not to tell them why I had been upset. I thought maybe it was a good idea to pretend like nothing happened. Instead I told them all about Sarah and the princess in the tower.

"Oh . . . uh . . . wow, Emma. A princess trapped in a tower? Hmm," said Sophia. She looked skeptical, like she didn't believe it was true.

"Emma, I have seen every princess movie ever made," added Shakira, "but here's the thing: Princesses aren't real! They're from fairy tales. Do you really think there's a princess trapped in a tower somewhere?"

"Hey, you never know," said Javier. "Princesses are real. They just don't live here in New York City. They live all over the world. And besides, in video games when you rescue the princess, you get to fight the fire-breathing dragon! I'm a dragon ninja!" Javier jumped into a ninja stance. "Count me in!"

"You guys," I responded, "I know it's not a real princess. But the girl who wrote this note *is* real and she asked for help. Fifteen years have gone by, and no one has helped her. If she says a 'princess' is trapped in a tower, we have to assume she's being serious. Something is wrong. And we're journalists. It's our job to help her."

"Maybe Emma's right. Maybe the riddle is trying to tell us something else," said Sophia.

"Yeah. This could be fun," agreed Shakira. "I'm in!"

We all decided. "Emma Is On the Air" was going to save the lost princess!

CHAPTER
FOUR

Find the Princess, Find the Tower

WE started hatching a plan, when Sophia thought of something important.

"Guys, what about the anonymous source? Remember? We still haven't solved that case."

Sophia was right. The last note I got from the anonymous source said *I need your help.* But we were never able to figure out who needed our help or why.

"I know," I said, "but what else can we do? We asked everyone at school if they sent the note; they all said no. We can't solve a problem and help someone if we don't know who that person is."

"Yeah, I know. I just hate leaving a case unsolved. That source has helped us out so many times. We owe it to her to return the favor," Sophia replied.

"Maybe the anonymous source will send us another note?" Javier suggested. "If the source really needs us, she'll reach out again."

"Good point," said Shakira. Ever since Javier and Shakira agreed to try out each other's toys, they've become really good friends. Shakira even tried on Javier's night-vision goggles—and wore them. *In public!*

"Thanks, Shakira." Javier smiled.

"That's right! Now back to work." I pulled out my purple reporter pad and wrote The Case of the Princess in the Tower.

Then I wrote clue #1:

A riddle was left inside an old book
that went missing for 15 years. "A
princess in a tower, locked away for
years. Please, someone save her.
Don't mind her floppy ears. I can't
tell you more. You'll have to find the
clues. She's trapped across the way
where the chirping babies snooze.
—Sarah Spellman, 30 Washington Way,
Seattle, Washington"

Then I wrote clue #2:

Library checkout card shows Sarah
Spellman was the last person to
check the book out in 2000.

And finally, clue #3:

Mrs. Myrtle, the school librarian, remembers Sarah. Sarah loved to read and didn't have many friends. Mrs. Myrtle didn't hear her talk about a princess in a tower.

"First step, let's look up that address in Seattle," I said.

We walked over to the computer in the library. Sophia typed in *30 Washington Way, Seattle.*

"A coffee shop?" Javier said, disappointed. That's what popped up on the screen: Jumpin' Java Coffee Shop.

"Why would a girl send a note from a coffee shop?" Shakira wondered.

"Look." Sophia pointed to the screen. "It says Jumpin' Java opened ten years ago. Sarah moved to Seattle fifteen years ago. Maybe she lived there before the coffee shop opened?"

"Maybe," I added. "But how can we figure that out?"

"I'm not sure," Sophia answered.

"Let's think. What else can we do?" I wondered.

"If you're going to save a princess from a tower," Javier said, "you have to find the tower!"

"Great idea! Let's go get some books about famous towers in New York City," said Sophia.

Most of the books we found showed skyscrapers, like the Empire State Building. That didn't seem like the right tower. Too tall. We found an apartment building in Brooklyn called the Clock Tower. That was a possibility, but we couldn't think of a reason why Sarah would need to save a princess in Brooklyn. In the Bronx, there was something called the Bell Tower. But it looked like you couldn't go inside it. None of the towers we found felt quite right.

"Library time is over," called Mrs. Myrtle. "Everyone line up."

Sophia stacked our books and put them on the cart.

"I'm sure there's more towers to find. I'll ask my mom when I get home," said Sophia.

We had all started gathering to form the line, when Mrs. Myrtle walked over to us.

"Oh, Emma, before you go, do you still have that book you found?"

"Yup yup! Right here."

"Oh, good. Make sure you hold on to it. It's looking like it doesn't belong to our school library after all. I can't find a record of it anywhere in the computer or in the old files. Can I take another look inside the book?"

"Sure." I handed her the book. She opened it up to look inside.

"Aha. That's what I thought. This book was checked out from the Jefferson Market Library down in Greenwich Village, not our school library. You know that library, don't you? It's the famous one—with the beautiful old clock tower."

Sophia, Shakira, Javier, and I all looked at one another. That was it. We found the tower.

CHAPTER FIVE

The Jefferson Market Library

AFTER school, I hurried to my room. As I waited for the interview with Mrs. Myrtle to load, I wrote my news report about our new case. It's funny—now that I've done so many reports, it's pretty easy to do the writing part. I just think about what I need to tell people and write it down. I don't know why it used to make me so nervous.

I was almost done writing my story. I had to add two more things.

Clue #4: 30 Washington Way is now the address of the Jumpin' Java Coffee Shop in Seattle.

And then,

Clue #5: The book was checked out from the Jefferson Market Library—which has a tall clock tower.

After I posted my news story to the school bulletin board, I ran downstairs for dinner and told my parents all about my new case.

"Oh, the Jefferson Market Library? I love that place," said Mom. "That's the library I used to go to when I was a little girl."

"Really?? Mom, we have to go!! Can we go now? Pleeeaaase?" I begged.

Luna jumped up onto the table and started begging, too. "Meeeeooooowww???"

She's such a good reporter's assistant! Always there when I need her.

"Luna, off the table," Papi said, giving her a light pat.

"Emma, be serious. We're in the middle of eating our dinner," Mom said.

"*Mi amor,*" Papi chimed in. "My love, let's finish our food first. *Primero come.* Then we'll talk about going to the Jefferson Market Library. Okay? *¿Está bien?*"

"Okay, fine, Papi. *Sí, está bien,*" I agreed. I swallowed my rice and beans and chicken as fast as I could without choking. Mom and Papi looked at me like I was being silly. Baby Mia started laughing. I just smiled with my mouth full and shrugged. I needed to get to that library!

After we cleared the table, Mom showed me what the library looked like on the computer. It kind of looked like a castle. A brick castle with a tall, pointy tower attached. It was amazing.

"This has to be it. When can we go?"

"To be honest, Emma, I'm not sure we can," Mom said. "It's all the way downtown, and we have so much to do on the weekends."

"But I have to! Please? Please?"

Mom sighed. "I'll try to figure it out. No promises."

The next day at lunch, I told everyone how I couldn't go to the library.

"No promises. That's what my mom said."

"Sorry, Emma," said Sophia.

"Yeah, that stinks," added Javier. "Now what should we do? The princess-eating dragons are

at the Jefferson Market Library. We have to get there somehow!" He started fighting invisible dragons in the lunchroom.

"Hey, Emma, can I borrow your shiny feather pencil?" asked Shakira. "I want to write down the name of the library again so I can look it up. I want to see where the princess is trapped!"

"Sure. It's in my backpack."

Shakira reached down the table to grab my backpack. She opened it up and started searching for my special pencil.

"Hey," she said. "I found something else. Look. I think it's another note from the anonymous source."

"What? Let me see!"

We all leaned over to see a folded piece of paper. Inside, there was a message written with pink ink!

"It *is* from the anonymous source! What does it say?" I asked.

"Read it!" Javier commanded.

"Hold on," Shakira said as she flattened the paper note. "It says, *Your enemy is your friend. The past is in the past. Make it right, and you'll find the princess. You'll help me, too.*"

"My enemy is my friend?" I said. "How will 'making it right' help the anonymous source? I'm confused."

"I don't get it," Javier said.

"Yeah, me neither," added Shakira.

"Let's think about it," said Sophia. "Who's your enemy?"

"My enemy? I don't know." I looked around the lunchroom. There was Melissa G. carrying her lunch tray over to the garbage can. Melissa? Was the source talking about Melissa?

"Maybe the source is talking about Melissa G.," Sophia said. She was reading my mind.

"Maybe," I said, "but what does Melissa G. have to do with the princess in the tower?"

"I don't know," said Sophia. Lunch was ending. Everyone started lining up for recess.

"Maybe you just have to make up with her to find out," said Javier as he leapt over to us, throwing his hands up like he was swinging a sword.

Ugh. That was the last thing I wanted to do—make up with Melissa G.

CHAPTER
SIX

My Enemy Is My Friend

WE got to the yard, and Javier was still pretending to fight dragons. This time, Adrian joined him, and they were throwing kicks and karate chops into the air together. I just stood in the corner of the school yard trying to figure out how to get to the library to find the princess.

I pulled out my reporter pad and wrote,

Clue #6: We got another note from
the anonymous source: "Your enemy

is your friend. The past is in the past. Make it right, and you'll find the princess. You'll help me, too."

What in the world did that mean? Shakira and Sophia were playing hopscotch, so I decided to forget about the clue and jumped in to play. I threw a piece of rock onto the number eight. I hopped up the chalk squares expertly, jumping right over the number eight. I never even touched the line. I hopped all the way back to the beginning. I proudly jumped out of the game and landed right next to Javier and . . . Melissa G.

"Whoa! Sorry. What are you guys doing here?" I said, startled.

"Emma, you *have* to talk to Melissa G. right now," said Javier. "Me and Adrian were fighting the Jefferson Market dragons, and Melissa heard us. She knows all about the dragons at the Jefferson Market Library! Melissa, tell her."

"No I don't!" Melissa G. responded. "Well, I know about the library, but I don't know about any dragons at the library."

"How do you know about the library?" Sophia asked.

"My grandmother lives downtown. She takes me there all the time. Actually, I'm a book volunteer on Saturday mornings. Why?"

"Really?" I said. Was the anonymous source really talking about Melissa G. after all?

"Yeah," Melissa said again, still looking unsure why we all cared so much.

"Oh, uh, we need to . . . I was trying to . . . oh, never mind."

"What Emma is trying to say," Sophia said, "is that we need your help."

"My help?"

Shakira nodded. "You know the big clock tower at the library? There's a princess trapped inside. Emma's trying to save her."

"It's not a *real* princess," I explained. "I mean, I'm not sure. Probably not. But there is a real girl who needs help and, yeah, we're trying to help her. But we have to get inside the library to do it. My mom won't take me."

"Oh. Okay . . . I guess I could help you. You could come with me next weekend. I volunteer in the children's section," Melissa said.

"Really?" I replied. I couldn't believe it.

Melissa shrugged. "I love princesses. And I know all about that library. Just tell me where you need to look." Suddenly she seemed excited. And *nice*! Was this the same person?

"That's the thing," I said. "We don't know

exactly where to look. I need to get into the clock tower and find the clues. That's what the riddle says anyway."

I showed Sarah's note to Melissa G.

"So you need to get into the tower to search for clues?" Melissa asked.

"Um, yes. Can you help me?"

"Actually, I'm not sure I can. No one's allowed in that clock tower. It's off-limits."

CHAPTER
SEVEN

Nellie Bly

OKAY, class, let's settle down," our teacher, Miss Thompson, announced.

We were back in our classroom after recess, and I still didn't have a plan. Melissa G. could get us into the library, but not the clock tower. And I was sure that was where my missing princess was.

Miss Thompson clapped to get our attention. "I'd like everyone to give a warm welcome to our guest speaker, Ms. Grace Patel from the New-York Historical Society."

I'd have to figure this out later.

"Hi, Ms. Grace," we said together.

"Grace is visiting to talk about a notable New Yorker from history."

"Hello, everyone," Grace said. "Today we are going to learn all about a very famous journalist. She was a pioneer in her time."

Suddenly my head perked up. A famous journalist? That's like me!

"Her name was Nellie Bly." Grace held up a black-and-white photograph of a woman from the olden days. She had dark hair pinned up on her head and a serious face. She had on one of those dresses women used to wear, with a really high collar.

"Nellie Bly covered all kinds of important news stories," Grace continued. "In fact, she even traveled around the world in a mere seventy-two days! That was a very big deal at the time.

Today—January 25—is the day she arrived back home more than a hundred and twenty-five years ago!"

"Wow," we all said together.

Grace handed the old photograph to Javier in the front row. Then we passed it around the classroom so everyone could see her up close.

"But Nellie Bly is most famous for an even more important news story," Grace continued. "It was an undercover investigation. Nellie Bly

was one of the first reporters to cover a story that way. She forever changed investigative journalism. Who can tell me what investigative journalism is?"

I raised my hand as high as I could.

"Yes?" Grace said, pointing at me.

"Investigative journalism is when a reporter has to do an investigation to find the answers for a news story. They have to do a lot of research and find out things no one knew before," I explained.

"That is exactly right! Excellent explanation," said Grace. "Nellie Bly helped to invent a special kind of investigation. She went 'undercover.' Does anyone know what that means?"

"I do!" Adrian called out.

"Adrian, we raise our hands," Miss Thompson corrected.

"Sorry," Adrian replied as he raised his hand.

"Okay, Adrian," Grace said, "what does *undercover* mean?"

"That's like when you're a police detective and you dress up as a bad guy in order to catch bad guys doing bad-guy stuff."

"Yes, that's one version of going undercover. And it's similar when a journalist goes undercover. They pretend to be someone else so they can get inside a place to see what's really going on there. It's usually a place where reporters aren't allowed. For Nellie Bly, it was a mental institution, a special kind of hospital."

"So she lied?" Javier asked—without raising his hand.

"She did lie," answered Grace. We all gasped. Grown-ups weren't supposed to lie.

"But she lied for an important reason," Grace went on. "Let me explain. In 1887, when Nellie Bly lived, hospitals weren't always as good as they are today. She heard about a particular hospital that did not treat patients very well. She thought that was wrong, and she wanted to know if it was true. The only way Nellie could know for sure was to see it for herself. But the hospital wouldn't let a reporter inside to see what was really going on. What could Nellie do?"

"Pretend to be a patient!" I called out.

"Emma?" Miss Thompson said with a look of disapproval. Oops. I forgot to raise my hand, too.

"Sorry," I replied.

"That's right, Emma!" Grace said. "Nellie Bly pretended to be a patient. She convinced the doctors that she was ill so she could sneak into the hospital and learn what it was like to be a patient there. Nellie saw for herself that patients were not treated well at all. They needed help. They needed someone to stand up for them.

"Nellie eventually told the doctors she was only pretending and left the hospital. Then she wrote a news story to tell the world about everything she witnessed. People were shocked and demanded justice for the patients in the hospital."

"Wow," said Javier. "Nellie Bly rescued people. She sounds like a superhero."

"Yes! She was like a superhero at the time," Grace agreed. "That kind of news story is called an *exposé*."

Just then, Shakira passed the photograph of Nellie Bly to me. I looked right in Nellie Bly's eyes. She looked so determined. She looked so fearless. She looked so . . . amazing.

"The most important thing a reporter can do is help people," Grace said. "And Nellie Bly did. She helped all the patients in that hospital by going undercover."

"Thank you so much, Grace," said Miss Thompson. "That was fascinating. Now, boys and girls, I want everyone to make their way to the rug for some math exercises."

I felt like I couldn't stand up. Nellie Bly was my new hero. She was fantastic! I wanted to be just like her. I wanted to help Sarah Spellman, and I knew exactly what I needed to do.

CHAPTER
EIGHT

Undercover

THAT Saturday, Melissa G.'s mom drove us both to the Jefferson Market Library.

"Have fun, girls," her mom called from the car. "I'll pick you up in about an hour."

"Thanks, Mom," Melissa called back.

We told Melissa's mom we were going to volunteer at the library. But really, I was there to go undercover. Just like Nellie Bly. It was the only way to get into the tower to find the clues to save the princess.

Melissa and I walked toward the front door of the library. The tomato-colored brick tower shot straight up into the sky like a castle. It was actually a little intimidating. But I had Sarah's book in my backpack, and I had a job to do. The princess was trapped in that tower somewhere.

We went straight to the children's section.

"Hello, Melissa," said a woman at the door. She was wearing a long green dress with a purple silk scarf tied around her neck. "Thank you for volunteering once again! Who's your friend here?"

"Hi, Millie!" Melissa smiled. I couldn't believe they knew her so well here. "This is Emma—she's here to volunteer, too. Emma, Millie is the head librarian."

"Nice to meet you," said Millie. "But I'm afraid we don't have any more room in the volunteer program right now. You're welcome to grab a

book and read while you wait for Melissa to do her work."

Melissa and I looked at each other. We both knew I needed to pretend to be a volunteer so it wouldn't look suspicious when we started searching for clues.

"Um ..." was all I could think to say. I certainly couldn't tell her I was actually a reporter on assignment. I was getting nervous our undercover plan wasn't going to work.

"Actually," Melissa chimed in, "Emma is my cousin. She's visiting us for a couple weeks while her parents look for an apartment in New York City. Her family is going to move here! She's dying to volunteer at the library so she can meet new friends. Can't she volunteer just this once?"

I couldn't believe what Melissa was saying. How'd she come up with that story? Maybe she really was a good actress!

"I don't know . . ." Millie said.

"Emma is a good worker. She won't be a bother—I promise! Please??" Melissa begged.

"Oh, all right."

"Yay!" we both screamed. I was so relieved.

"Actually, we do need help with a new book recycling program," Millie said. "We're looking for ways to reuse old books that have been damaged, especially the baby board books. Maybe Emma can help with that?"

"That's perfect!" I shouted a little too loudly. "I mean, great. I'll do it."

"Can I help Emma with the board books, Millie? They might be heavy," Melissa pointed out.

"Yes, that's fine. Go ahead. You'll have to gather all the damaged books. Talk to Louis the custodian," Millie instructed. "He can get some boxes for you. Just down the hall and make a right. Louis's office is in the clock tower."

What a stroke of luck! Melissa and I looked at each other with excitement. We started heading down the hallway toward the tower office. This was our chance to get inside and look around. We made a plan. Melissa was going to talk to Louis the custodian and distract him, while I snooped around the tower searching for clues.

We continued down the hallway, and it started getting darker. There weren't many windows in this part of the library. It was even a little creepy. Suddenly I was feeling nervous.

We were almost at the tower—and I noticed something. Not some*thing*, some*one*. There was a trail of crumbs. We were being followed.

"Melissa, wait," I told her as I looked behind us. "Did you see that?"

"See what?" she asked, turning around.

"I could've sworn I just saw someone following

us down the hallway. And look at the crumbs on the floor."

"I don't see anyone. Those crumbs were probably there before we got here. Come on, we have to hurry. We need to get the boxes and figure out a way to snoop around inside the tower."

"Okay, I know. Let's go."

We walked a little farther, and we could see a big brown door that looked like it was connected to the tower. We were just about there when . . . *CRASH!* Something crashed to the ground and made a huge noise. Melissa and I both screamed.

CHAPTER
NINE

What Are You Doing Here?

A **PILE** of books had fallen off a shelf and onto the hallway floor. Someone had knocked them over and was buried beneath them. I was too scared to dig through the books to find out who it was. The person started moving a little bit, and I saw a small patch of dirty-blond hair peeking out between the books. There was a single hand sticking out, holding what looked like a jelly sandwich.

"Adrian?! Is that you?" I called.

"Yes," he answered softly. His voice was muffled by the books on top of him.

"What are you doing here?" Melissa yelled as she ran over to pull the books off him.

Adrian looked straight at me and said, "I'm here to help." Then he took a bite of his sandwich.

I started feeling weird. And embarrassed.

"You want to help me?" The butterflies in my stomach started jumping out of control.

"Sure, why not?" He looked straight at me with a smile. "I got hungry waiting for you guys to finish your volunteer work. I was expecting some action."

"Oh," I said back. But before I could say anything more, Louis the custodian came out of his office.

"What's this ruckus?" he asked, scowling.

"Oh, hi," Melissa answered. "You must be Louis. Sorry for the mess. We're volunteers at the library. All *three* of us ..." Melissa looked at Adrian and rolled her eyes. He stuffed the rest of his jelly sandwich in his mouth.

"Millie sent us here to get boxes for the book recycling program," Melissa went on. "Adrian slipped and knocked over some of these books in the hallway. Sorry about that."

"In that case . . . come to my office," Louis said. "I have some boxes in the back."

Adrian quickly put the books back on the shelf, and we all followed Louis into his office, just inside the tower.

"I think the boxes are in this back closet," Louis said.

"Okay," Melissa responded. She followed him into the back, then gave us a signal to start snooping. I winked back at her.

"We only have a couple minutes," I whispered to Adrian. "We need clues that lead to the princess."

He looked excited. "What kind of clues?"

"I'm not really sure," I said. We looked around the office. I noticed a window on the other side. There was a perfect view to a construction site across the street. Just past the window was a doorway. I walked through, and Adrian followed.

There was a huge spiral staircase that went all the way up the top of the tower. Bingo.

"Let's go," I said.

"Are you sure?" Adrian said. I could tell he was a little nervous. I was, too.

"Yes. The princess is trapped in the tower. That means we climb the tower."

We started marching up the stairs. So many stairs! Finally we reached a landing and another open doorway. It was a small room that looked kind of like a lounge where you go to take a break. There was a small table with a TV on top, an old sofa, a small refrigerator, and another small table with a deck of cards on it.

"This must be where the custodian takes his breaks," Adrian said.

"I think you're right. Quick, look for . . . well . . . clues!"

Adrian and I searched the room. We couldn't find anything. I took the riddle out of my pocket and read it again, *"A princess in a tower, locked away for years. Please, someone save her. Don't mind her floppy ears. I can't tell you more. You'll have to find the clues. She's trapped across the way where the chirping babies snooze."*

"What does that mean?" asked Adrian. "I don't hear any chirping."

"I'm not sure. Birds chirp, right? There aren't any birds in this tower."

Then we heard Melissa. She was talking extra loud.

"Gee, thanks, Louis! Ten boxes are great! But I need just ONE more . . ."

"We gotta go," Adrian whispered.

"Ugh . . . okay. But we haven't found anything yet." I started looking around the room in a panic. I spotted a closet. I ran over to it.

"What's in there?" Adrian asked, looking over my shoulder. It was just a bunch of junk. But in the back corner ... I saw a pink backpack. I picked it up. Stitched on the front pocket were the letters *S.O.S.*

CHAPTER
TEN

S.O.S.

I **OPENED** the pink backpack, looking for a clue. Inside was nothing but a pair of binoculars.

"What are these for?" I wondered.

"I don't know, but we have to go. *Now!*" Adrian said.

I took a moment to look through the binoculars. All I saw was the same room—just

71

really big. I spotted the window and ran over, looking out—but there was nothing there. Just a huge pine tree. And that same construction site. I could see bulldozers and dump trucks. Looked like they were working on a big project.

Suddenly I felt Adrian grabbing my arm.

"Come on!" Adrian pulled me down the stairs.

We ran down as fast as we could and got back to the office just as Melissa grabbed the last box from Louis.

"I think we're all set," Melissa said, sounding relieved. She gave us a *let's go right now* look. We each grabbed some boxes and left.

That Monday, I brought the pink backpack to school with me to show everyone. At lunchtime, everyone crowded around our table. It was me,

Melissa, Adrian, Sophia, Javier, Shakira . . . and even Molly and Lizzie. I looked around and I couldn't believe it. A week ago, I had no friends, and now I had more than enough. It made me feel special.

"Did you find the princess?" Shakira wanted to know.

"Not exactly."

"But we're getting closer!" Adrian said with excitement.

"What did you find?" Sophia asked.

"This," I said as I plopped the bag on the table.

"What's that?" Javier asked.

"It's a backpack," Molly answered.

"It's pink," Lizzie added.

"It says S.O.S.," Sophia noticed.

"Yep," I replied.

"What does that mean? That the person who

owns this bag is in danger? She needs help?" Sophia asked.

"That's what we thought at first," I said. "But Melissa figured it out after we got home."

"Yup!" she said proudly. I took out the *Bridge to Terabithia* book so she could show them. Melissa pulled out the library card. "Javier, read what it says," she instructed.

"*October 17, 2000. Sarah O. Spellman.* So? I don't get it."

"Sarah O. Spellman!!" Sophia yelled excitedly. "S.O.S. are Sarah's initials! So this is her backpack?"

"It is! We found Sarah's backpack," Adrian announced proudly.

"Great," Shakira said. "But is the princess inside it or something?"

"Well, no," I answered. "Only these binoculars. I don't know what it means. But I do know we need to go back undercover at the library!"

Everyone nodded.

"Here's the thing. Since I'm undercover, we can't do any more news reports about this story until it's over. Got it? No one can say a word!"

"Got it," they all said. I looked around the table and felt really proud. It was like I had an entire news team helping with the investigation.

"And one more thing," I added. "I want to say sorry to everyone for the way I acted last week. Especially to Melissa G. I don't know why I said those mean things on the playground. I think I was just feeling frustrated . . . and crazy things just jumped out of my mouth by accident. I didn't mean it, and I shouldn't have said it. Forgive me?"

"Puh-leeze," said Adrian. "We were never mad."

"Yeah," said Melissa with a smile. "No problem here."

Sophia, Shakira, and Javier all smiled at me.

I pulled out my purple reporter pad and my shiny feather pencil so I could update my clues.

Clue #7: Sarah O. Spellman left her
   pink backpack in the custodian's
   office in the tower. It has her
   initials, S.O.S.

Clue #8: Inside was a pair of
   binoculars. Out the window I saw a
   big tree and a construction site.

I wasn't sure if the tree and the construction site had anything to do with the princess, but I figured I should make note of them anyway.

Lunchtime ended a couple minutes later, so we got up from our table to head outside for recess. I was walking behind Adrian on my way to the school yard when I noticed something. There was something sticking out of Adrian's back pocket. It was pink. Why would Adrian have something pink in his pocket? I looked a little closer. It was a pen. Adrian had a pink pen . . .

CHAPTER
ELEVEN

Adrian's Pink Pen

I RAN to catch up to Adrian. Then I grabbed his arm and pulled him outside to the school yard and over to the side.

"Why are you pulling me?" he asked.

I reached behind him and grabbed the pen out of his pocket. I held it up so he could see.

"This is why. A pink pen?"

"Oh, um, I...I...um..." Adrian stammered. "It's my sister's. I—I lost my other pens."

"Adrian, come on. Really?"

He looked down without answering. And then I knew it.

"Ever since I became a famous news reporter I've been getting notes from an anonymous source," I said to Adrian. "And the anonymous source always writes with pink ink. And pink hearts. Javier even found a grape jelly stain on one of the notes. And *you* eat grape jelly sandwiches for lunch every day! 'Fess up. You're the anonymous source, aren't you?"

"Okay, fine. It was me," Adrian admitted in a quiet voice. He kept looking down at his feet, shifting around like he was nervous.

"So why did you write me all those notes? Why did you use a pink pen and write with little hearts?"

"I wrote with a pink pen because I didn't want you to figure out it was me. I thought if I added hearts you would think a girl wrote the notes."

He was right. I did think it was a girl. That was silly. I should have known better. Everyone knows that pink can be for boys and girls.

"And I guess I just wanted to help you. It all started with Sophia's missing costume. Remember when you asked me if I had seen it? If I knew what happened?"

"Yes," I answered.

"I said I hadn't seen the costume, but I saw Molly pick it up off the floor and put it in her bag. I didn't want to tell you because girls are weird and they get mad about stuff. I didn't want to get Molly in trouble. But I didn't want you guys to lose the contest, either. So I wrote you a note."

"Wow. What about the tambora drum?"

"By then, I was watching your show all the time. It was pretty cool. When I saw the drum at Alyssa's house, I wanted to tell you. We live in the same apartment building, and our moms are friends. My mom sent me over there to borrow some laundry detergent. Alyssa's mom told me it was in the closet, first door down the hall. I opened the door, but it wasn't the closet, it was Alyssa's room. She wasn't there, but the tambora drum was. I saw it."

"Why not just tell me? Why did you have to be anonymous?"

"Because . . . I don't know. I just didn't want to get anyone in trouble."

I nodded. "What about the next note? You said you needed my help, and then you disappeared. What happened?"

"I just really wanted to be on the team. I wanted to be your friend. So I figured I'd make up a case so we could work together. And maybe be friends that way."

I started getting that funny butterfly feeling again in my tummy. I liked the idea that Adrian wanted to be my friend.

"But why make up a story? Why not just ask to be my friend?"

"I don't know. I sort of thought you might not want to be my friend because I'm friends with

Melissa G. I've known Melissa G. forever. Since we were babies. I thought you might not like me since you don't like her."

Suddenly I felt guilty again. I *was* mean to Melissa G.

"I like Melissa G.," I said. "Well, I like her now. Now that I know her better."

"But you didn't like her then," Adrian continued. "I figured I could convince you to like me if you were helping me with a case. But I couldn't think of one. I didn't really need help with anything mysterious. My life was too boring. Then you started working on the case of the lost princess. I knew Melissa would be the perfect person to help you get to the tower. And maybe I could help this time. So ... I ... ah ... wrote you another note."

"Yes, I remember." I pulled the note out and

read it out loud, *"Your enemy is your friend. The past is in the past. Make it right, and you'll find the princess. You'll help me, too."*

"Yeah. By making up with Melissa, you'd help me by being my friend."

My face was turning red again. I didn't know what to say. Suddenly recess was over. Adrian and I went back inside for class. We didn't talk about it again. We were friends now—that's what mattered.

CHAPTER
TWELVE

Time to Save the Princess

I **DECIDED** not to tell anyone about Adrian. Papi says a real reporter never reveals her source's identity. And now Adrian and I really were friends. I wasn't going to do anything that might hurt his feelings or embarrass him.

The next Saturday morning, we went back to the library for our volunteer jobs. Mom and Papi knew I was going to the library with Melissa—but no one knew we were undercover.

Adrian was coming back with us again. He insisted I needed help snooping—and maybe he was right. It's hard to keep track of time when you're hunting for clues. Javier, Shakira, Sophia, Molly, and Lizzie decided to come, too, to watch and be the lookouts. We told all our parents we were forming a study group. Javier's mom said we needed a chaperone since there were so many kids, so she came along, too. So did Sophia's dad. Papi said that was a good idea.

"Wow, *mija*, I can't believe you got your whole class interested in the Jefferson Market Library," Papi said that morning while I was eating my breakfast.

"They thought it was cool there might be a princess trapped in the tower. Javier thinks there's dragons up there! But we're just going to study." It felt wrong to lie to Papi, but I couldn't tell him I was undercover! He might tell the librarian and ruin our investigation.

"And what about your case? Is there a princess in the tower?"

"Eh," I answered. "I'm not really sure. I mean, there's no such thing as princesses trapped in towers anymore."

"Oh, I see. Well, have fun with your friends."

We all arrived at the library. Melissa and I were collecting board books again. Some of them still had baby drool on them. Ick. In the back of the room, Sophia, Javier, Shakira, Molly, and Lizzie all sat at a table. Adrian was just behind them, pretending to look for a book. We had to get back to the tower. Melissa came up with a plan.

"Millie," Melissa called. "Um ... this board book looks like it can be fixed. Can I go to Louis's office to get some tape, please?"

"Sure," Millie replied. "We should always try to save a book! Hurry back."

"Okay," Melissa said. She and I started walking toward the tower. Adrian put back the book he was pretending to read and followed us. Everyone else tried to hide their sneaky smiles as they watched us leave.

We got to the tower, and Melissa went with Louis to find the tape and fix the book. Adrian and I ran right toward the stairs and back up to the lounge.

"Okay, now what?" Adrian asked.

"I don't know . . . Look around some more?"

There didn't seem to be anything else. I found myself back over by the window looking at the big tree and the construction site. Why did Sarah need those binoculars? What was she looking at? I glanced up at the ceiling and noticed a handle.

"Adrian, look."

He walked over to me.

"A door," he said, pointing.

"A door in the ceiling?"

"Yeah. My uncle has one of those in his house. That's how you get to the attic . . . You just have to pull it down."

Adrian pulled the table over to the window and climbed on top of it. He reached up to grab the handle on the ceiling and pulled it down. The door opened and down came a set of

stairs. There was another floor. We were about to climb up the stairs when we heard Melissa G.

"Wait, Louis, wait—"

But it was too late. Louis the custodian walked into the lounge and stared right at us. He didn't look happy.

CHAPTER
THIRTEEN

Uh-Oh

WHAT in the world is going on here?" Louis asked, his voice angry and his hands on his hips.

"Um ... well ..." Melissa stammered. This time she didn't know what to say.

"Who gave you permission to come up here? This tower is off-limits—especially for children. And that staircase you pulled down—that's dangerous. You could get hurt!"

Louis was so mad. I just stood there. Frozen. We didn't know what to do. We were in big trouble. Then Adrian spoke up.

"We're sorry," Adrian said.

"Who are you?" Louis asked.

"I'm Adrian."

"He's a volunteer, remember?" Melissa said.

"No, no I'm not," Adrian answered.

"You're not?" Louis asked. He looked even madder.

"No. It's time to be honest."

"What?" I asked. What was Adrian doing?

"Emma, we have to tell the truth. You and I both know the answer to the riddle has to be up those stairs. Louis is the only one who can help us. We need to tell him what's really going on."

"Okay," I said. But I was pretty nervous.

Louis looked impatient. "I'll ask one more time: What is going on here?"

Adrian took a breath and said, "We're not really volunteers."

"We're undercover," I explained.

Melissa, Adrian, and I told Louis the whole story. We even showed him the book, the riddle, and Sarah's backpack and binoculars.

"Huh" was all he said.

"Yeah, we're really sorry," Melissa said.

"We just need to help out Sarah," I added. "She never had any friends when she was a little girl. We're trying to be her friends now and help her save the princess!"

"Hmm," Louis grunted.

I was getting even more nervous. What was Louis going to do to us? He might kick us out, get us in trouble, and keep us from finding the princess forever!

"Well," he continued slowly, "I didn't have many friends as a kid, either."

"You didn't?" Adrian asked.

"Nope. I was pretty lonely. I wish I had some

friends like you. That's pretty nice what you're trying to do."

"Thanks!" we said.

"I don't know anything about this lost princess. That sounds . . . well . . . a little strange. But I suppose it couldn't hurt to look."

"Really?" I screamed.

"Okay, settle down. Yes, really. *But* you have to follow my lead. I will take you up to the top of the tower *if* you do exactly as I say. Got it?"

"Got it!" we shouted together.

Louis walked over to the ceiling door Adrian had pulled down. He pulled it down a little farther and locked it into place so it was secure.

"Follow me." Louis began to climb the stairs, and we went right behind him. We were in a much smaller room this time. It was more like an attic. We had to duck our heads because the slanted ceiling wasn't tall enough. There was just enough room for a small window.

"Look around—but don't touch anything unless I say it's okay."

"Got it," I replied. And then I heard something. Adrian heard it, too, and we looked right at each other.

"Chirping," he said. We could hear birds chirping. We were getting closer.

"Louis," I said, "can you open the window for us? We need to see where that chirping is coming from."

"Okay." Louis opened the window. We looked out and saw the very top of the enormous pine tree across from the tower. The chirping was even louder.

"I hear the birds, but I don't see anything," Adrian said.

"I know," Melissa chimed in. "Emma, hand me the binoculars."

I pulled the binoculars out of Sarah's backpack. Melissa took them and looked out the window.

"Guys, you have to see this," she whispered.

"What is it?"

"Just look."

Melissa handed me the binoculars and I looked. It was amazing! I could see an entire bird family in a nest. But not just any bird family. It was an owl family. There was a mama owl and a daddy owl and three little baby owls. It was the cutest thing I'd ever seen. The babies were chirping, but the parents were sleeping. *That's right*, I thought. *Owls sleep during the day.* At least, grown-up owls do.

I handed the binoculars to Adrian so he could see, too. Even Louis couldn't believe it.

"My goodness. I had no idea that owl family was living up here. That's just incredible," Louis said. "I've never seen anything like it."

"Guys, you know what this means?" I said.

"What?" Adrian asked.

"We're really close. Remember, the princess is 'trapped across the way where the chirping babies snooze.'"

"Right!" Melissa replied.

"We're across from chirping babies. The princess is here somewhere."

We looked around the room again. And in the corner near the window, I spotted a pillow. It was pink. I lifted it up and screamed.

"I found her! There she is. It's the lost princess!"

CHAPTER
FOURTEEN

Found Her!

I BENT down and picked her up. It was a princess, all right. A princess puppy doll with floppy ears. Just like Sarah said in her riddle: "don't mind her floppy ears." The puppy was wearing a silly pink dress and had a little purse. The purse had words stitched on it that read, "My precious princess."

"A toy? A toy puppy? We went through all that to rescue a toy puppy princess?" Adrian sounded annoyed.

"It may be just a toy to you," I answered. "But it meant a lot to Sarah. And we found her."

"Hey, Emma," Melissa G. said.

"Yeah?"

"There's something in the princess puppy's bag."

Melissa reached inside the purse and pulled out an envelope. Inside the envelope was a ring—and a note.

"Read it," Adrian said.

"For my special niece Sarah. You will always be my princess. Love, Uncle Peter."

"Peter? Uncle Peter?" Louis the custodian asked.

"Yeah, that's what it says," Melissa said.

"Oh my goodness. That must be Peter

O'Mally. He was the custodian here a long time ago. It must be fifteen years now. I took over for him. Very nice man. And come to think of it, yes, I remember he had a niece who came to the library with him. She always carried a little toy and read books all day long. I might have even seen that princess puppy."

"Wow!" I said. "We have to get it back to her. And the ring. They must have both been very special."

"I bet they were," Louis answered. "Sarah must have sat up here when her uncle was working. I bet she sat on that pillow and looked out the window with her binoculars."

"She must have," I said. "Even back then, there were probably birds in that tree. She was right across from where the chirping birds snooze!"

Suddenly we heard a loud noise outside the window. It sounded like a bulldozer. I still had the binoculars, so I used them to see if the noise woke up the owl family. They were still sleeping. Then I looked down to the ground and saw something awful.

"Oh, no!" I gasped. "The tree! They're going to knock down the tree!"

"What?" Louis looked out the window. We started yelling for the construction workers to stop. If the tree fell down, the little owl babies would be hurt! But the workers couldn't hear us.

"What should we do?" Melissa cried, looking scared.

"Hurry! We have to go right now!" Louis walked toward the stairs.

He was right. But first I started shooting video of the owl babies. We had to show everyone what was up in the tree. Once I was done, I slipped my phone in my pocket, and we all raced down the stairs.

No one knew about the owl nest except for us. The nest was so high up in the tree, you couldn't see it unless you were at the very top of the tower.

We got to the main lobby, and we ran past Javier and Sophia and everyone else without saying a word. They all followed right behind, confused and concerned.

"Wait, Emma, stop!" called Sophia's dad.

"Yes, hold on a minute," added Javier's mom. "Where are you running off to?"

"There isn't much time to explain," Adrian said.

"We were at the top of the tower and found an owl family," I said in a rush. "And the babies are chirping, but the construction workers are going to tear the tree down. We have to save them!"

"You were at the top of the tower? What

were you doing up there?" Sophia's dad wanted to know.

"I gave them permission," Louis said, winking at me. "Emma, show them the video of the owls." I handed my phone to Sophia's dad, and they all crowded around to see.

"Oh my goodness," Javier's mom said. "Let's not waste any more time! Let's go save those owls!"

CHAPTER
FIFTEEN

Emma to the Rescue

WE all dashed out of the library. I had my camera phone out as our whole group ran across the street. I recorded while we yelled to the construction workers.

"Stop! Stop! Don't tear the tree down! There's an owls' nest up there! The baby owls will die! You have to stop!"

Suddenly all the workers stopped what they were doing and looked in our direction. We made it across the street, and Louis started explaining to the workers what was going on.

"Show them the video," Louis said to me.

I pressed play and showed them the nest.

"Oh, man," the worker said. "We didn't know those guys were up there. Well, we'll have to tell the boss about this." He walked away  and started talking with a group of workers at the scene.

"What does that mean? Will the boss make them stop?" I asked.

"I'm not sure, Emma. I hope so," Louis said with a worried look on his face.

I knew what I had to do. I still had the puppy princess in my hand. I gave it to Melissa G. so I could focus. I had a news report to finish.

I found my microphone in my bag and plugged it into my camera phone. I gave Sophia the camera, and she pointed it right at me. Shakira came over and fixed my hair. Javier kept the crowd away so the tree could be seen behind me. I started to feel a little nervous. I looked over at Sophia.

"Go ahead, Emma. This is the most important story we've ever done. The owls are depending on us. You can do it."

Sophia was right. I looked right into the camera and just started talking about what was happening. I didn't have time to write my news script—I had to just go. So I did. I told the whole story about the owls in the tree. Then I edited my story to show the video of the owls' nest all the way up in the tree. I included video of the construction workers and how they were planning to tear the tree down. Finally my report was done, and I posted it to the Internet.

A couple minutes later, Sophia's dad's phone rang. It was Papi.

"Papi, I'm so glad you called. We need help!"

"Emma, I just saw your news report. Is this true? Are those owls really in danger?"

"Yes! We're trying to convince the workers not to tear down the tree, but I don't know what they're going to do."

"Okay—stay there. I'll be right over."

Papi showed up twenty minutes later—and he wasn't alone. He came with a photographer from his newspaper, the *New York Herald*. Behind them, another car pulled up. It said *Animal Control* on the side. Then *another* car pulled up—a police car! And then, behind the police car, a fire truck arrived!

"Hi, *mija*," Papi said as he walked over to all of us. "Looks like you have a breaking news story on your hands. I called everyone I could think of. They all agree we have to save the owls. No one should tear down that tree."

The newspaper photographer who came with Papi started taking pictures of the tree and the construction workers. The police officers and the firefighters walked over to the workers, and they were all standing in a circle talking and looking up.

"Papi, I'm so nervous. Is your newspaper going to do a news story on this?"

"We sure are," Papi replied. "You uncovered a heck of a story, *mi amor.* Good stuff."

"I guess. I'm just so scared the baby owls will be hurt," I said, holding Papi's hand. "Who's that behind you?"

Papi looked around. Someone was walking toward us. It was a woman in a gray suit with a blue shirt. She looked pretty serious.

"Well, well, well," Papi said. "*That* is a city councilmember. Her name is Felicia Simmons. She's very powerful. Emma, your story got the attention of Councilmember Simmons. Well done."

"Hello, Miguel, good to see you again," Councilmember Simmons said to Papi. Miguel is his real name.

"Hello, Councilmember. I want to introduce you to my daughter Emma. She's the one who discovered the owls."

"Yes, I heard all about it. Good work, Emma. I saw your report. Don't worry. We're not going to let anything happen to that owl family."

"Thank you," I replied, smiling.

Councilmember Simmons walked over to the group of people talking.

"I just heard from the mayor's office," she told them. "No one is allowed to touch this tree. That's an order from the mayor."

I started screaming and jumping. We all did. We did it! The owls were safe!

"I'm very proud of all of you," Papi said after we calmed down a little. "This is what journalism is all about. Telling people things they need to know—and helping those who need it. If it weren't for you all, no one would have known about the owls. Good work.

"But there's one more thing we need to talk about," Papi said, becoming serious.

Uh-oh.

"Sophia's father told me how you snuck up to the top of the library tower. You know better than to do that. It's off-limits for a reason."

"But we were undercover!" I explained. "Just like Nellie Bly. We had to get up there to save the princess."

"I know," said Papi. "But Nellie Bly was a grown-up when she went undercover. You are all still kids, and you can get hurt. You got lucky this time. And you ended up doing a good thing. But, please, no more undercover assignments. Got it?"

"Okay," I said.

"Mr. Perez," Louis said, stepping in. "I'm the custodian at the library, and I'm in charge of the tower. I caught Emma snooping up there and told her how dangerous it was."

"I see," Papi said.

"But then I saw what they were doing and how smart and determined they were, and I decided to help them. I made sure no one was in any danger."

"Well, thank you, Louis. I really appreciate that."

"It was no problem. She's a good kid."

"You're right about that," Papi agreed.

Louis winked at me. I think he was proud.

CHAPTER
SIXTEEN

One More Interview

THE next day, I was preparing my final news report on the case of the princess in the tower. But I still had some questions. Like, why did Sarah leave her princess puppy there to begin with? And how did the *Bridge to Terabithia* book end up at my school library? We found the princess, but it didn't make any sense.

I told Papi about all my questions and he agreed to help me track down Sarah Spellman for some answers. Papi started by looking up the address in the riddle. Then he called the local newspaper in Seattle, and together they were able to figure out that Sarah Spellman lived on Washington Way five years before Jumpin' Java Coffee Shop opened. They even found her new address. She was still in Seattle! Papi called her, and she was so thankful we found her puppy and ring, she agreed to do an interview with me.

"Hi, Sarah! It's me, Emma," I said once I saw her pop up on my computer screen. "Can you see me? I can see you!" I was interviewing her over the Internet.

Sarah Spellman was not a nine-year-old girl anymore. She was a grown-up now. And she looked happy.

"Yes, hello, Emma! I can see you. Thank you so much for finding my ring! And my stuffed puppy. My uncle Peter gave me the ring as a going-away present before we moved, and I was so sad to have left it behind."

"Sarah, that's what I want to know. Why *did* you leave it behind? And how did your book end up at the P.S. 387 library?"

"Well, P.S. 387 was my school, too, before my family moved to Seattle! The book was returned there by mistake—it should have gone back to the Jefferson Market Library. When I was a little girl, I spent every weekend at that library with my uncle Peter. He was the custodian there. My parents were both busy working and going to college on the weekends, but I didn't mind. I loved all the books."

"Did you play up in the tower?" I asked.

"Well, I wasn't supposed to, but I would sneak up to the very top and look out the window with my binoculars. I used to pretend I was a princess trapped in a tower!" Sarah smiled at me. "One day, I spotted an owl building a nest in the tree. Soon there were two owls, and then came the eggs. No one knew about them but me because they were so high in the tree and never flew around in the daylight."

"That's just like the owl family we found. They never flew around during the day. But, Sarah, why did you leave the princess behind?"

"When my parents told me we were moving to Seattle, I knew I would miss my little owl family," Sarah told me. "I decided my little princess puppy should stay there in the tower to watch over them. It was only after we moved that I realized I left my ring in the princess's pocket. I wanted it back so badly, but I was afraid I would get in trouble if I told my parents what happened. I was never supposed to go up into the upper level of the tower by myself!"

"We weren't, either," I said. "Oops!"

Sarah laughed. "Well, Emma, I wasn't sure what to do. But then I discovered that I had a library book I forgot to return. I knew this was my chance to get the ring back. I wrote the note and put it in the book. I gave it to my mom to send back to the library in New York City. I was hoping a kid would find my note and then find my ring—a kid like you, Emma! But after the book got lost, I figured I'd never see that ring again. Until I got a call from your father—fifteen years later!"

"Wow. What a story, Sarah. I'm so glad I found your ring!" I told her.

"Me too! But I'm even more pleased to hear you saved the owls! They must be the grand-children of the owls I met when I was a kid. I left my princess there to protect them—and in a way, she did. Thanks to you!"

Papi and I were both amazed by Sarah's story. I included the interview in my news report and posted it one last time. I had officially solved the case!

"I'm really proud of you, *mija*," Papi said. He picked up the newspaper page I had pinned to my bulletin board. "Look at you. A real reporter on the front page of the paper."

The morning after we saved the owls, we made it into the newspaper. There was a picture of me and the whole news team on the front page!

"You really are famous now," Papi said. "You are officially a famous TV news reporter. Just like you wanted."

"I'm proud of you, too," Mom said, coming into my room.

Luna jumped on my lap. "Meow!"

EMMA IS ON THE AIR

Even baby Mia clapped her hands and said, "EMMA FAMOO EMMA FAMOO."

"Yeah, I guess I am famous. *Soy famosa*," I replied. "But you know what, I don't think I really care about being famous anymore."

"Oh, no? How come?" Papi asked.

"Well, there are so many more important things to care about. I didn't have time to worry about being famous when I was doing my investigation. We had to work really hard to find all our clues. Just like Nellie Bly, we had to be a voice for the voiceless. All this time we've been helping people. We helped Javier with his wormburger. We helped Sophia with her costume. We helped all the mangulina dancers find the tambora drum. And now we've helped the owl family keep their nest and Sarah get her ring back. I think that's the part I like the best. The helping part."

"That's my girl. *Eso es mi niña*," Papi said, giving me a huge hug.

I have to admit, being in the newspaper is pretty cool. I know it's not the most important thing in the world . . . and it's not the reason you should become a journalist . . . but I still do love being FAMOUS! Ha-ha!

I got up and started doing the famous jumpy dance with Luna. This time Mom, Papi, and baby Mia got up and danced with us!

EMMA'S TIPS FOR NOT-BORING NEWS!

1. **Keep your eyes open.** You never know when one news story will lead you to another. The second story may be even more awesome than the first!

2. **Get creative—carefully!** Sometimes you have to find different, even undercover, ways to get your news report done. Just make sure you're not hurting anyone, and ask your parents before being a sneaky sneakster!

3. **Make everyone your friend.** When someone is super mean and you think they will never ever be nice, don't get mad. Try being nice to them first. A good news reporter turns everyone into a friend!

4. **Don't give up!** Some news stories might feel impossible. That's just because you don't know all the facts yet. Keep going and it will all come together.